MAX'S CASTLE

Kate Banks   PICTURES BY Boris Kulikov

Frances Foster Books

Farrar Straus Giroux ■ New York

For Max. *And Peter.*

For Max. *And Andre.*

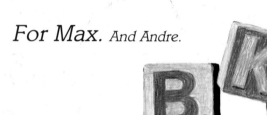

Text copyright © 2011 by Kate Banks
Pictures copyright © 2011 by Boris Kulikov
All rights reserved
Distributed in Canada by D&M Publishers, Inc.
Printed in July 2011 in China by South China Printing Co. Ltd.,
Dongguan City, Guangdong Province
Designed by Lili Rosenstreich
First edition, 2011
1 3 5 7 9 10 8 6 4 2

mackids.com

Library of Congress Cataloging-in-Publication Data
Banks, Kate, 1960–
    Max's castle / Kate Banks ; pictures by Boris Kulikov. — 1st ed.
        p.   cm.
    Summary: When Max finds a box of long-forgotten toys, he builds a kingdom
filled with adventures for himself and his two brothers.
    ISBN: 978-0-374-39919-1 (alk. paper)
    [1. Play—Fiction.   2. Toys—Fiction.   3. Brothers—Fiction.   4. Knights and
knighthood—Fiction.   5. Imagination—Fiction.]   I. Kulikov, Boris, 1966–   ill.   II. Title.

PZ7.B22594Mas 2011
[E]—dc22

                                                                        2010021388

MAX reached into a box under his bed.
He was looking for something.

When he found it, he put it in his pocket.
"Hey, what's that in your pocket?" asked
Max's brother Benjamin.
"It's something amazing," said Max.
He opened and closed his fist (in his pocket).
"What is it?" said Karl. He was Max's other
brother.
"It's something marvelous," said Max.
He wiggled his fingers (in his pocket).
"Well, show us!" demanded his brothers.

Max took his hand from his pocket and opened it slowly. "It's a block," he said.
On one side of the block was a letter.
"What's so great about that?" asked Karl.
"Aren't you too old for that?" asked Benjamin.
"No," said Max.

He pulled the box from under his bed.
Inside were more blocks of different colors, shapes,
and sizes.
There was another box filled with toys, and another
with a dinosaur skeleton.
"What are you going to do with those?" asked
Benjamin.
"I'm going to make a castle," said Max.

He began by building the WALLS.

Then he built some HALLS.
Pretty soon the castle had many rooms.

"May I have a room?" asked Karl.

"Sure," said Max.

He put some DINOSAUR BONES in Karl's room.

"That's my old BUGLE," said Karl. "I wondered where it was."

"I want a room, too," said Benjamin.
Max took MORE BONES and made BEN'S ROOM.
"There's my old monkey," said Benjamin.

Max constructed a MOAT around
the castle.
"We need a BOAT," said Benjamin.
"Okay," said Max.
"Can I take a ride?" asked Benjamin.
"Okay," said Max. "All aboard!"

But they hadn't gone far when they spotted a ship.
"PIRATES!" Benjamin cried.

"I can turn those PIRATES into RAT PIES," said M

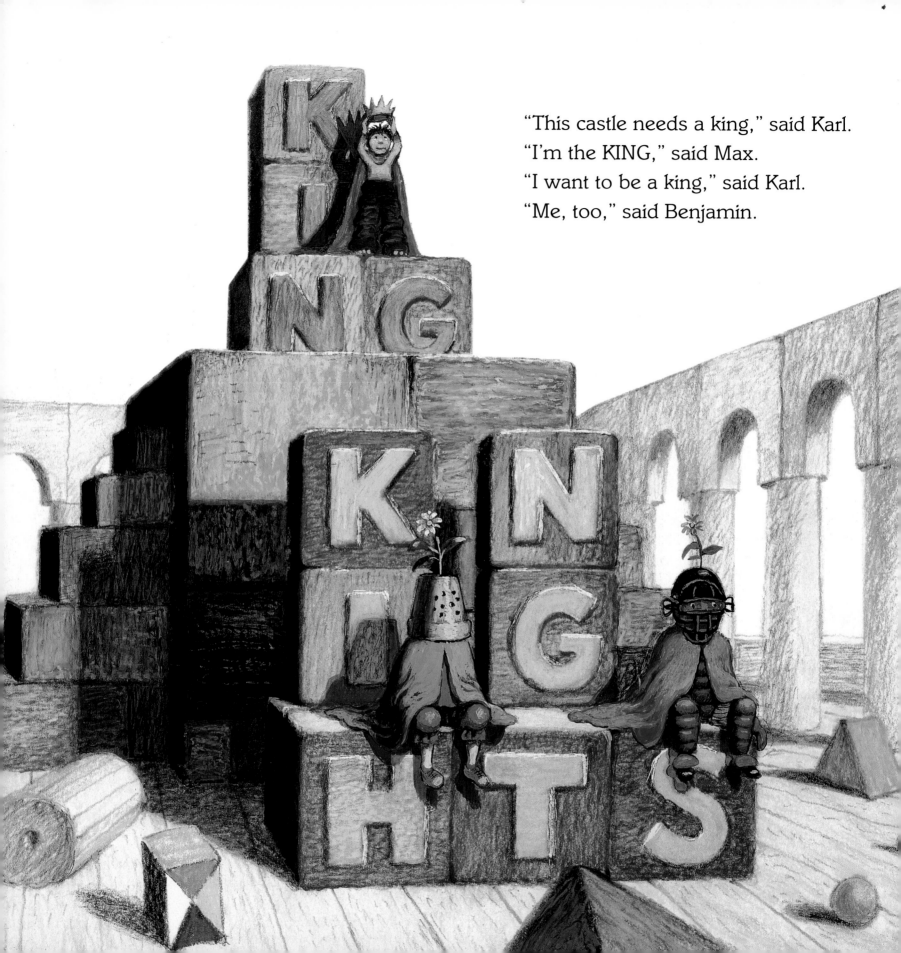

"This castle needs a king," said Karl.
"I'm the KING," said Max.
"I want to be a king," said Karl.
"Me, too," said Benjamin.

"You can be KNIGHTS," said Max.
"In every KNIGHT there's a KING."

Benjamin picked up a sword and waved it in the air. "On guard," he said.

"There are no weapons in my kingdom," said Max. "We don't BATTLE. We BABBLE. So what do you have to say for yourself?"

Benjamin was silent.
"I will turn your SWORD into WORDS," said Max.
"And this SPEAR will become PEARS."

"And your GUN into a BUN," said Karl.
"With JAM or HAM," said Max.

Max tossed Karl and Benjamin some blocks:

HILKGEOTNLGVINE

LONG LIVE THE KING.

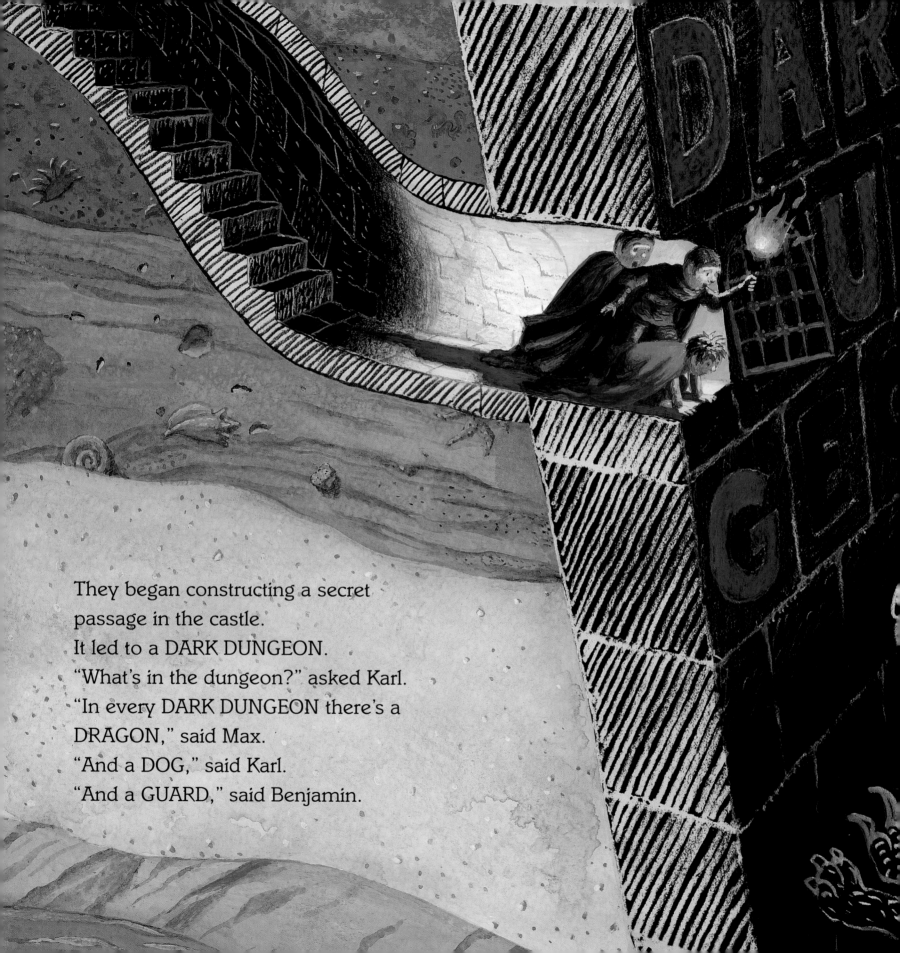

They began constructing a secret
passage in the castle.
It led to a DARK DUNGEON.
"What's in the dungeon?" asked Karl.
"In every DARK DUNGEON there's a
DRAGON," said Max.
"And a DOG," said Karl.
"And a GUARD," said Benjamin.

Suddenly the castle was under siege.
"It must smell the rat pies," said Karl.

Max moved quickly and soon the
BLACK CAT was a BLOCK CAT.
But not before it had knocked
over some CHAIRS, and sent
Max, Benjamin, and Karl tumbling
down the STAIRS.

They landed in the dark dungeon.
"I can't see a thing," said Benjamin.
"This is a CATASTROPHE," said Karl.
Max was turning letters around,
looking for a way out.

"We don't have the right words to get out of here," said Benjamin.
"In every CATASTROPHE there's HOPE," said Max.
"And there is a STAR," said Karl.

"Look," said Benjamin. "It's a chest. I wonder what's inside."

"It's locked," said Karl. "If only we had a key."

"I see a key," said Max.

He took the KEY from MONKEY and opened the chest.

They all peered inside.

"Uh-oh," said Max. "In every DARK DUNGEON
there's an ADDER, too."

"What's an ADDER?" said Karl.

"A snake," said Benjamin.

The snake began to uncoil. It lifted its head.

"We need a snake charmer," said Benjamin.

Karl took his BUGLE and began to play.

The snake rose into the air, twisting and turning.

"If I could just borrow that L," said Benjamin.
He took the letter from BUGLE, and the
music stopped.

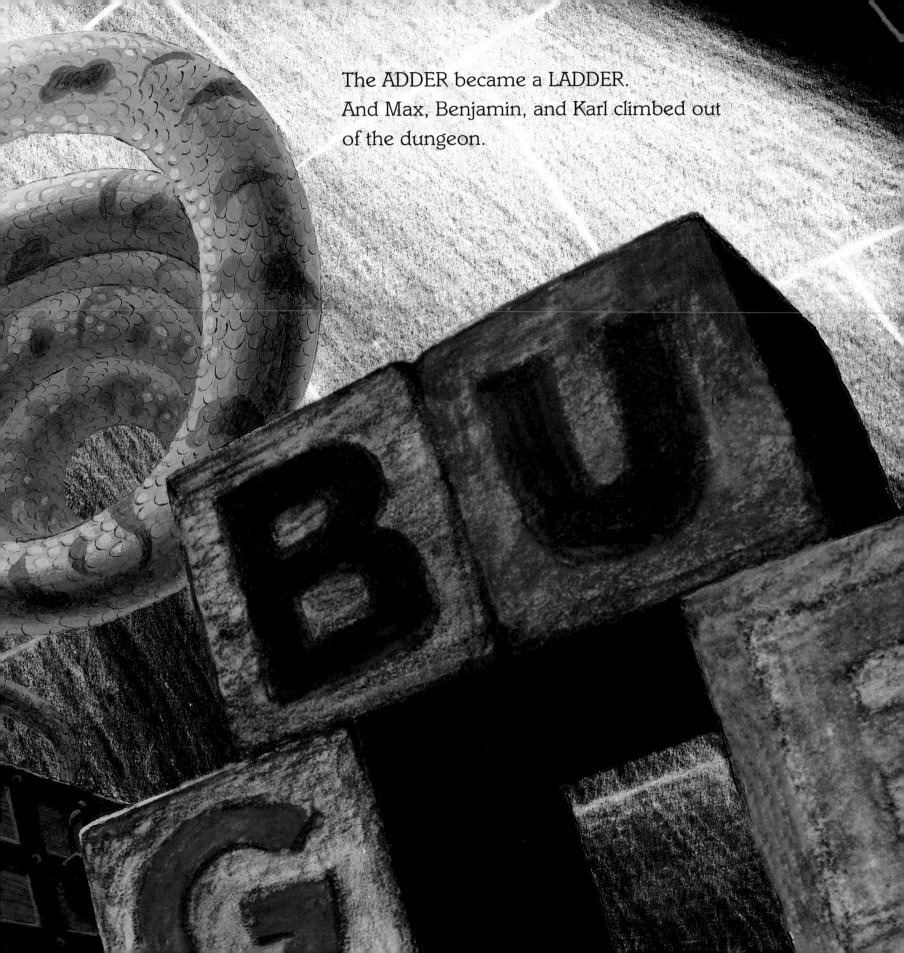

The ADDER became a LADDER.
And Max, Benjamin, and Karl climbed out
of the dungeon.

The knights followed the king back to the great hall.
"In this DRAWER is a REWARD," said Max.

"Usually the knights get a DAMSEL," he said. "But I will give you MEDALS instead.

And a HORSE, of course."

Then the king called his knights to
the round table.
And for their loyal FEATS he organized
a FEAST.
From the castle TAPESTRY he made PASTRY.
And from the PARAPETS he made TEA.

Then with all the leftovers he made SPAGHETTI.

"Long live the king!" said Karl and Benjamin.
"And long live his knights," said Max.